Our Twitchy

To John Roe and linden days – KG
To Yvonne with love – MM

OUR TWITCHY

A RED FOX BOOK 0 09 943419 9

First published in Great Britain by The Bodley Head,
an imprint of Random House Children's Books

The Bodley Head edition published 2003
Red Fox edition published 2004

1 3 5 7 9 10 8 6 4 2

Red Fox Books are published by Random House Children's Books,
61– 63 Uxbridge Road, London W5 5SA,
a division of The Random House Group Ltd,
in Australia by Random House Australia (Pty) Ltd,
20 Alfred Street, Milsons Point, Sydney, NSW 2061, Australia,
in New Zealand by Random House New Zealand Ltd,
18 Poland Road, Glenfield, Auckland 10, New Zealand,
and in South Africa by Random House (Pty) Ltd,
Endulini, 5A Jubilee Road, Parktown 2193, South Africa

THE RANDOM HOUSE GROUP Limited Reg. No. 954009

www.**kids**at**randomhouse**.co.uk

A CIP catalogue record for this book is available from the British Library.

Printed in Singapore

Our Twitchy

Kes Gray & Mary McQuillan

RED FOX

Twitchy was watching a butterfly
being a butterfly. "Mum," he said, "why
don't butterflies hop like me?"
"Because they're butterflies," smiled Milfoil.
"Dad," said Twitchy, "why don't
you and Mum hop like me?"

Sedge looked at Milfoil. Milfoil looked
at Sedge. "Sit down, Twitchy," said
Sedge, "there's something you need to
understand."

Twitchy sat down and took a bite out
of his carrot.

"The reason we don't hop like you
is . . ." said Milfoil.

"I'm not your Bunnymum," said Milfoil.
"And I'm not your Bunnydad," said Sedge.

Twitchy twitched his nose and blinked.
Milfoil tried to explain. "Twitchy, your
Bunnymum and Bunnydad brought you to
us when you were tiny. They couldn't look
after you because they already had sixteen
little ones to feed. They wanted someone to
love and care for you properly, so we said we
would, and we did, and we have ever since."

"I don't understand," whispered Twitchy.
"If you're not my Bunnymum and my
Bunnydad, who are you?"

"I'm a cow," said Milfoil.

"And I'm a horse," said Sedge.

Twitchy blinked again. "But you can't be," he said. "Bunnies live in burrows. We all live in a burrow." "It isn't really a burrow, Twitchy, it's an empty train tunnel. We wanted it to be like a burrow," said Milfoil.

"But bunnies eat carrots all the time. We eat
carrots all the time," said Twitchy.

"It's very dark in the train tunnel, Twitchy,"
explained Sedge. "We eat carrots to help us see
in the dark."

"I still don't understand," said Twitchy.

"Come with us," said Milfoil and Sedge.

Twitchy followed Milfoil and Sedge down to the banks of the river.

"Look into the water, Twitchy. What do you see?" asked Milfoil.

Twitchy stared long and hard at the reflections before him.

"I see two pairs of big brown eyes that always twinkle when they look at me. I see two great big kind smiles that always make me feel happy," said Twitchy.

"I see the two best bunnies in the world."

"But, Twitchy, look again," said Milfoil. "You have long floppy ears. We have much shorter ones."

"You have a white fluffy tail. We both have long dangly ones. Your fur is soft and grey. Ours is shiny and brown," said Sedge.

Twitchy lowered his eyes to the ground. "I've never noticed before," he whispered.

"We can't possibly be your Bunnymum and your Bunnydad, can we, Twitchy?" said Milfoil.

Twitchy twitched his nose, burst into tears and ran away. Away from the river, away from Milfoil and Sedge, as away as away would take him.

Milfoil and Sedge ran after him.
   They called his name from the highest
hills and down into the deepest burrows.
They asked every bird and animal they
met if they knew where Twitchy might be.
But nobody had seen him.
Twitchy had gone.

It began to get late, and it began to get dark,
too dark to see. When Milfoil and Sedge
started bumping into trees, they knew they
would have to give up the search.
With big sighs and heavy hearts,
they slowly turned for home.

They were two fields
away from home when
Sedge and Milfoil suddenly
pricked up their ears. A strange
sound was coming from the direction of
the train tunnel. It was faint and very
trembly, like a 'moo', or was it a 'neigh'?
Milfoil and Sedge looked at each other and
galloped for home.

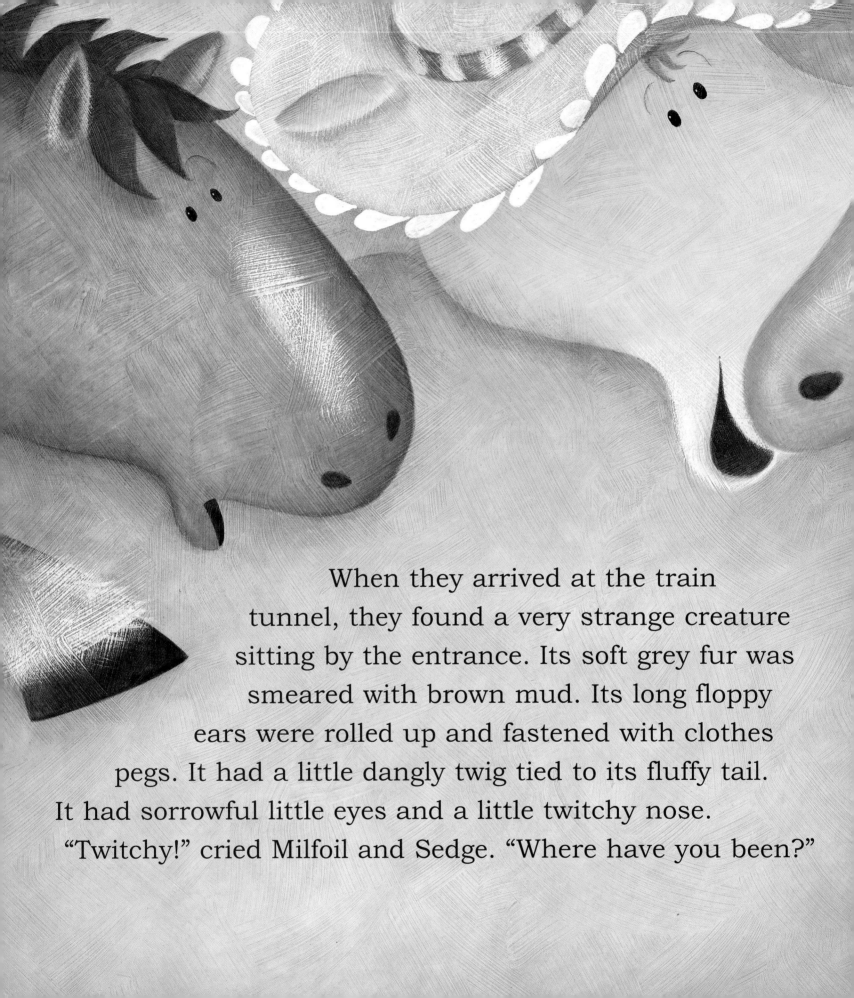

When they arrived at the train
tunnel, they found a very strange creature
sitting by the entrance. Its soft grey fur was
smeared with brown mud. Its long floppy
ears were rolled up and fastened with clothes
pegs. It had a little dangly twig tied to its fluffy tail.
It had sorrowful little eyes and a little twitchy nose.
"Twitchy!" cried Milfoil and Sedge. "Where have you been?"

"Moo," whispered Twitchy.

"Neigh," whispered Twitchy. "I can change. I promise I can change. I can be a cow or a horse. Please be my real Mum and Dad." His voice trembled.

Milfoil bent down and gently licked the brown mud from Twitchy's fur. Sedge carefully removed the clothes pegs from Twitchy's ears and the twig from Twitchy's tail.

"We are your real Mum and Dad, Twitchy," smiled Milfoil. "We've always been your real Mum and Dad. We might not be bunnies, but we've always loved you and cared for you just the same. We don't want you to change!"

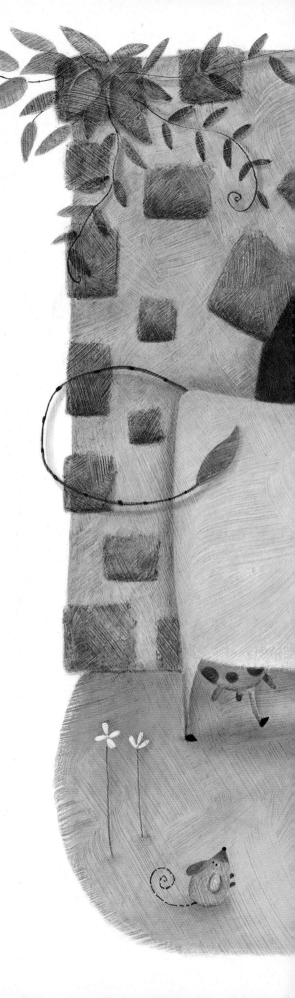

"You'll always be our Twitchy," said Sedge.
Twitchy twitched his nose and gave a little hop.
"That'll do for me!" he said.

Ten more hops into the train tunnel, Twitchy turned and shouted at the top of his voice: "What's for tea, Mum and Dad? Mum and Dad? Mum and Dad?!"

He liked the sound of his voice when it echoed inside the tunnel.

Milfoil and Sedge laughed, and shouted happily back: "Carrots, son! Carrots, son! Carrots, son!"

They felt more like a family than ever before.

C

More books you might enjoy:

Illustrated by Mary McQuillan

Who's Poorly Too?
by Kes Gray

Squeaky Clean
by Simon Puttock

Who Will Sing My Puff-a-Bye?
by Charlotte Hudson

Written by Kes Gray

Billy's Bucket
illustrated by Garry Parsons

The Daisy books
illustrated by Nick Sharratt:

Eat Your Peas
Really, Really
You Do!
Yuk!